KU-468-568

Carlo
and the Really Nice
Librarian

WALKER BOOKS
AND SUBSIDIARIES
LONDON • BOSTON • SYDNEY • AUCKLAND

Jessica Spanyol

One day Dad
took Carlo and
Crackers to
the new library.

The
Library

Fiction

Children's Books

Welcome

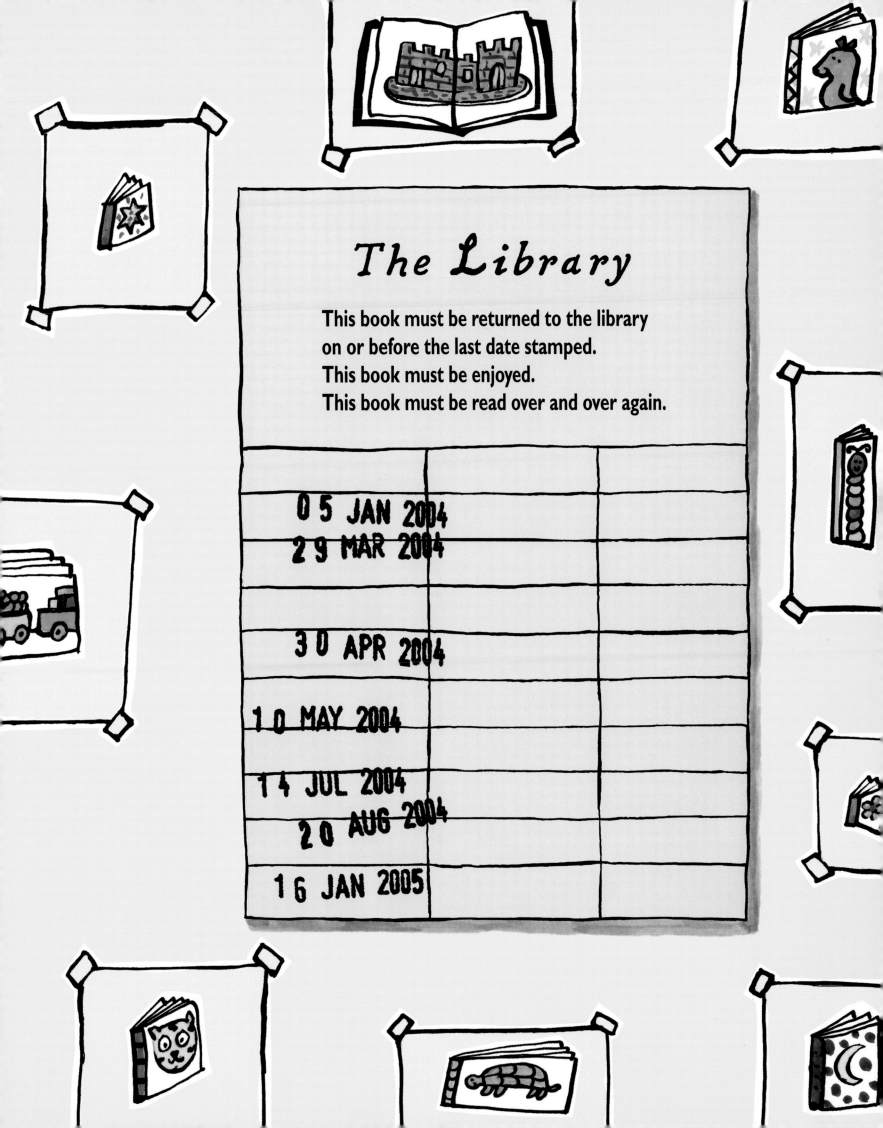

The Library

This book must be returned to the library
on or before the last date stamped.
This book must be enjoyed.
This book must be read over and over again.

05 JAN 2004		
29 MAR 2004		
30 APR 2004		
10 MAY 2004		
14 JUL 2004		
20 AUG 2004		
16 JAN 2005		

for my
mum

my Dad

John

Jill

and
for
Aunty
Jempy

ROTHERHAM LIBRARY
SERVICE

B511022

Bertrams	24/05/2010
JF	£7.99
BSU	

First published 2004 by Walker Books Ltd
87 Vauxhall Walk, London SE 11 5HJ

This edition including DVD published 2008

2 4 6 8 10 9 7 5 3 1

© 2004 Jessica Spanyol

The right of Jessica Spanyol to be identified as author/illustrator of this work
has been asserted by her in accordance
with the Copyright, Designs and Patents Act 1988

This book has been typeset in LN Spanyol

Printed in China

All rights reserved. No part of this book may be reproduced,
transmitted or stored in an information retrieval system in any form
or by any means, graphic, electronic or mechanical, including photocopying,
taping and recording, without prior written permission from the publisher.

British Library Cataloguing in Publication Data:
a catalogue record for this book is available from the British Library

ISBN: 978-1-4063-1542-4

www.walkerbooks.co.uk

"Wow!" said Carlo when he saw all the books.

Dad called after Carlo, "I'm going to be just around this corner if you need me."

The library was very impressive.
There were colourful posters.
There were chairs
with wheels on.

And there was the longest
desk Carlo had ever seen.
"Come on, Crackers,"
said Carlo.

"Wheee!"

Books In
. The Red Balloon
. Bugs
. My Kite
. Daisy

"Hello, I'm Mrs Chinca.
What's your name?"
"Carlo," whispered Carlo.
"And who is this?"
asked Mrs Chinca.

"That's Crackers. He's my cat."
Mrs Chinca the librarian
seemed a bit scary.

"What sort of books do you like, Carlo?" asked *Mrs Chinca*.

"All sorts," Carlo said quietly.

"Very good. Well, let me tell you about our library books. Come on, Carlo, **follow me.**"

"This is a lovely bedtime story," said *Mrs Chinca.*

"Just look at these beautiful pictures, Carlo."

"And this is a very exciting read."

"ROAR!"

said *Mrs Chinca*
when she saw
the lion.

Carlo laughed
so much he got
his tail into
a tangle!

Next, *Mrs Chinca* asked Carlo to help her with her work. "You have such a lovely long neck, Carlo. Could you put these books on the top shelf?" Carlo really liked helping *Mrs Chinca*.

WALKER BOOKS is the world's leading
independent publisher of children's books.
Working with the best authors and illustrators
we create books for all ages, from babies
to teenagers – books your child will
grow up with and always remember. So…

FOR THE BEST CHILDREN'S BOOKS,
LOOK FOR THE BEAR

There was a tiny
bite-sized bit missing!

"Mrs Chinca really does love her books,"
laughed Carlo.

B51 051 022 4

ROTHERHAM LIBRARY & INFORMATION SERVICE

STAFF USE ONLY   WAT

WATH

-3 AUG 2018

This book must be returned by the date specified at the time of issue as the DATE DUE FOR RETURN.
The loan may be extended (personally, by post, telephone or online) for a further period if the book is not required by another reader, by quoting the above number / author / title.

Enquiries: 01709 336774

www.rotherham.gov.uk/libraries